# MOUNTAINS

# MOUNTAINS

**PETER MURRAY**

THE CHILD'S WORLD®, INC.

## PHOTO CREDITS

Comstock: cover, 2, 6, 9, 10, 13, 15, 16, 19, 20, 23, 24, 26, 29, 30

Library of Congress Cataloging-in-Publication Data

Murray, Peter, 1952 Sept. 29-
Mountains / Peter Murray.
p.   cm.
Includes index.
Summary: Describes different types of mountains and how they are formed.
ISBN 1-56766-279-X (hadcover)
1. Mountains—Juvenile literature.  [1. Mountains.]
I. Title.
GB512.M87   1996
910'.9143—dc20                      96-5433 [B]
                CIP
                        AC

# TABLE OF CONTENTS

In 1991, the body of a man was found in the mountains known as the Alps, near the border of Austria and Italy. He was frozen into a block of ice. The man was dressed in leather and woven grass. He carried a bow and arrows, a stone dagger and a copper ax. Scientists studied the body. It was 5,300 years old!

The frozen man was nicknamed the Iceman. But who was he really? Was he a shepherd searching for a lost sheep? A trader who had lost his way? Why would the Iceman have climbed 10,000 feet up the side of a mountain?

The Iceman was found in the *Alps*

When you look up at a skyscraper, do you ever wonder what it would be like to take an elevator to the very top? Do you ever see a bird sitting high in a tall tree and wonder what it sees? Have you ever sat on a hill and felt as if you could see forever?

Human beings have always been fascinated by high places—and what could be higher than a mountain? What would it be like to stand atop the highest places on our planet? Maybe the Iceman wanted to find out.

View of Andes from above

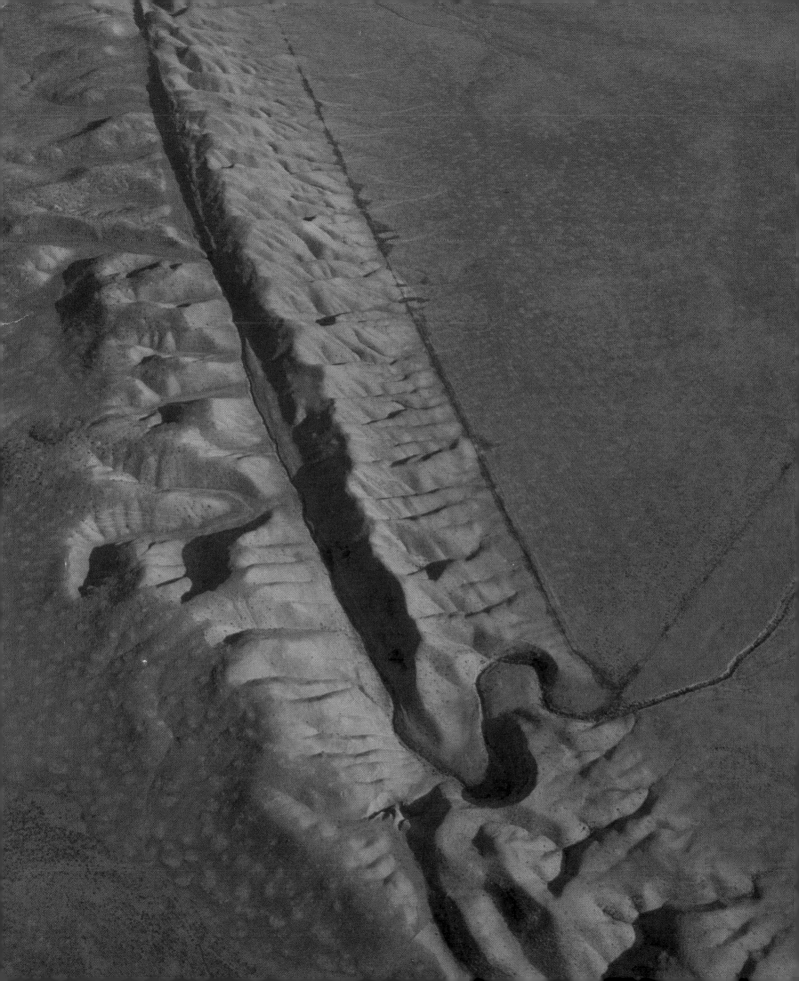

When you look up at a mountain, it looks as though it has been there forever. But it hasn't! Our planet is not a solid ball of rock. The earth's surface is constantly changing. Think of our planet as a gigantic soft-boiled egg. Its rocky shell is about fifty miles thick. This shell, or **crust**, is broken into several large pieces. They are called **crustal plates**. These plates fit together like pieces of a jigsaw puzzle. They also float like rafts on a sea of hot, half-melted rock called the **mantle**.

A fault line shows the edge of a crustal plate

# WHAT ARE FOLD MOUNTAINS?

The crustal plates are slowly moving. They push against each other and pull apart. They might take a hundred years to travel an inch! When two plates collide, the rock folds and crumples. Over millions of years, the **collision zones** rise to become mountain ranges. These are called **fold mountains**.

Fold mountains form when two plates collide

The highest mountains on our planet are fold mountains. The Himalayas (him-uh-LAY-uhs) of central Asia have fourteen mountains that are over 26,000 feet high. The tallest is Mount Everest. It is 29,028 feet high!

Mount Everest was first climbed in 1953 by Sir Edmund Hillary and Tenzig Norgay. The air was so thin near the top that they had to breathe oxygen from a bottle. A hundred million years ago, when dinosaurs roamed the earth, the Himalayas did not even exist. We know this because scientists have found remains of sea creatures high in the Himalayas. The Himalayas were once the bottom of an ocean!

Mount Everest is the highest mountain on Earth

# WHAT ARE VOLCANIC MOUNTAINS?

Fold mountains take millions of years to form. The Himalayan Mountains are still rising. But not all mountains grow slowly. **Volcanic mountains** can shoot up quickly.

When the Earth's crustal plates move, cracks can form deep underground, all the way down to the mantle. Melted rock called **magma** fills the cracks. It rises up through the crust toward the surface. When magma spills out onto the Earth's surface, we call it a **volcano**. As more magma spills out, the volcano becomes higher. Eventually, a volcano might become a mountain.

Magma spills out from a volcano

In 1943, a farmer in Mexico was working in his field when a crack appeared in the ground. Sparks and glowing rocks flew into the air, setting nearby trees on fire. The next morning, a pile of ash and lava 35 feet high stood in the middle of his field. And it was still growing! A few days later, a cone-shaped volcano almost 500 feet tall covered the farmer's fields. It was named Parîcutin (par-uh-koo-TEEN).

Today, Parîcutin is a volcanic mountain 1,000 feet high. Some volcanic mountains are even higher. Mount Kilimanjaro (kill-i-mun-JAR-o) in Africa is a volcano more than three miles high.

Lava from a volcano flows across the ground

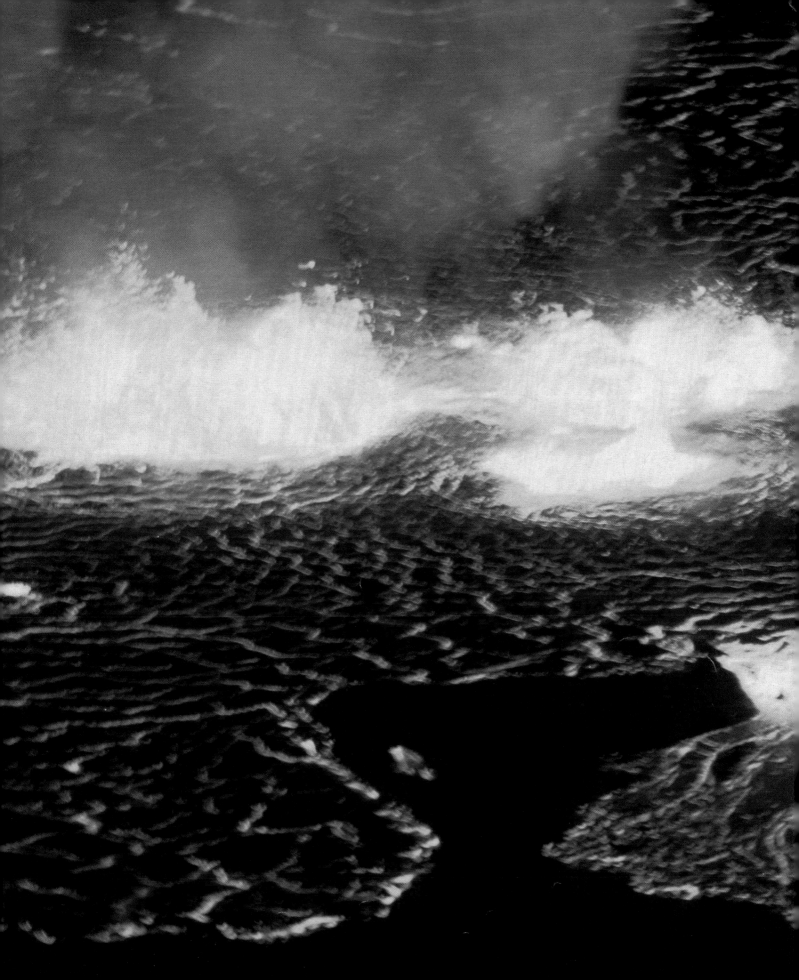

# WHERE ARE THE LARGEST MOUNTAINS?

The tallest volcanic mountains on Earth don't look very tall at all. That's because we can see only the very tips of these volcanoes. The rest of them are under the ocean. The largest underwater mountains are as tall as the Himalayas!

The Hawaiian Islands are actually the tips of giant undersea volcanoes. They are still slowly growing.

The tip of an undersea volcano forms an island in the ocean

The tallest mountain we know about is called *Olympus Mons*. Olympus Mons is a volcano as big around as the state of Arizona. It stands ten miles high.

Scientists would love to visit Olympus Mons, but it is very hard to get there. It's on Mars!

Olympus Mons, on Mars, is the tallest mountain known to people

What is it like to climb a mountain? Mountaineers will tell you that it is different every time. The tallest mountain in Scotland is 4,400 feet high. It can be climbed in a single day by a lone climber with no special equipment.

The ice-covered peaks of the Himalayas are a greater challenge. Those who try to climb the Himalayas' greatest peaks must be ready for sudden storms, landslides, bitter cold, and air too thin to breathe. A Himalayan climb can take months of planning and weeks of climbing.

Ice-covered peaks are difficult to climb

# WHAT IS LIFE LIKE IN THE MOUNTAINS?

In the Andes Mountains of Peru, you might start your climb in a hot, sticky rain forest filled with chattering monkeys and screeching parrots. As you climb higher, the wide-leafed rain forest plants disappear. Soon you are looking up at tall pine trees. The air becomes cool. Soon, there are only a few scattered bushes growing on the mountainside. There are also patches of snow. You might see a *llama*, or a soaring *condor*.

People who live in the mountains are used to change. As you move up or down a mountain, you see different plants and animals. In the Catalina mountains of Arizona, a half-hour climb can take you from a hot, cactus-covered desert to a snow-covered pine forest. The weather also changes quickly in the mountains. When moist air from the sea swoops up the sides of a mountain range, it quickly cools and condenses into rain or snow.

The climate in mountain areas changes quickly

Men and women have climbed all of Earth's greatest mountains. Every year, another 500,000 people go mountain climbing. They climb to see whether they can do it. They climb to enjoy the beauty of the mountain. They climb so they can stand at the very top and look out over the world.

What do you think the Iceman was doing on that mountain in the Alps? Did he die while he was trying to get to the top? Or had he already been there?

A mountain climber enjoys the beauty of the mountains

# GLOSSARY

**collision zones (co-LI-zhun zones)**
Places where the earth's crustal plates run into each other. Mountains often form along collision zones.

**crust (krust)**
The rocky shell that covers the earth. It is about fifty miles thick.

**crustal plates (KRUS-tull plates)**
Huge pieces of the earth's crust that fit together like pieces of a jigsaw puzzle. Mountains sometimes form when these plates run into each other.

**fold mountains (FOLD MOUN-tuns)**
Mountains that form where the earth's crustal plates push together. The earth's rocky crust bends and pushes up to form mountains.

**magma (MAG-muh)**
Melted rock that lies deep inside the earth.

**mantle (MAN-tull)**
Half-melted rock that lies underneath the earth's rocky crust.

**volcanic mountains (vol-CAN-ik MOUN-tuns)**
Mountains that form from volcanoes. As melted rock spills out of the volcano, it builds up higher and higher and forms a mountain.

**volcano (vol-KANE-o)**
A place where melted rock from inside the earth forces its way to the surface and spills out.

# INDEX